THE SHADY TREE

To my grandson, Burhan John Hitz

Henry Holt and Company, LLC
Publishers since 1866
175 Fifth Avenue
New York, New York 10010
mackids.com

Library of Congress Cataloging-in-Publication Data
Names: Demi, author, illustrator.
Title: The shady tree / Demi.
Description: First Edition. | New York : Henry Holt and Company, 2016. | A Companion to: The empty pot. | Summary: Ping returns
    and deals with the selfish Tan Tan, who owns a beautiful house and a beautiful shady tree, but who does not share, so Ping turns Tan
    Tan's greed into his own gain, but remains true to his generous nature.
Identifiers: LCCN 2015034855 | ISBN 9781627797696 (hardback)
Subjects: | CYAC: Folklore—China. | Sharing—Fiction. | BISAC: JUVENILE FICTION / Fairy Tales & Folklore / Country & Ethnic. |
    JUVENILE FICTION / Social Issues / Values & Virtues. | JUVENILE FICTION / People & Places / Asia.
Classification: LCC PZ8.1.D38 Sh 2016 | DDC 398.2—dc23
LC record available at http://lccn.loc.gov/2015034855

Our books may be purchased in bulk for promotional, educational, or business use.
Please contact your local bookseller or the Macmillan Corporate and Premium Sales Department at (800) 221-7945 ext. 5442 or by
e-mail at MacmillanSpecialMarkets@macmillan.com.

First Edition—2016 / Designed by Eileen Savage
The artist used watercolor and mixed media to create the illustrations for this book.
Printed in China by RR Donnelley Asia Printing Solutions Ltd.,
Dongguan City, Guangdong Province

10 9 8 7 6 5 4 3 2 1

THE SHADY TREE

DEMI

Henry Holt and Company • New York

Once upon a time in China, there was a very rich boy named Tan Tan who lived in a very big house by the side of the road.

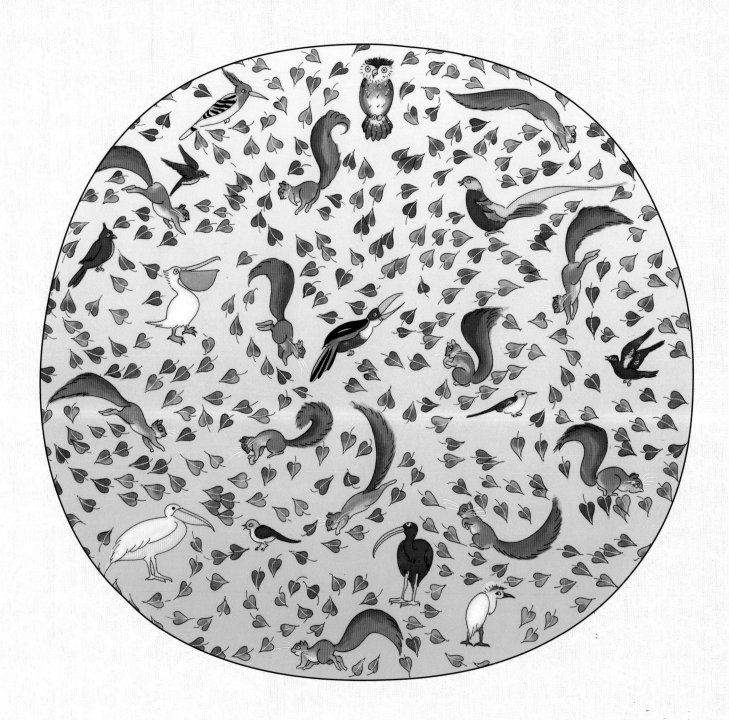

The house was shaded by a very big tree

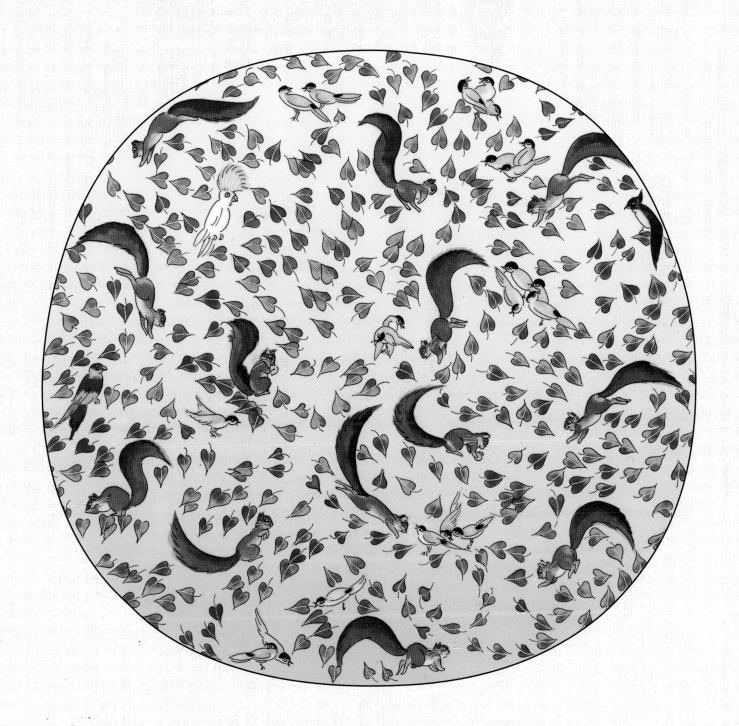

where birds and animals loved to play.

Tan Tan also loved to play in the shade of the tree with his very expensive toys.

One afternoon, a very poor boy named Ping came and sat down under the tree. Tan Tan did not like this at all.

"Get up! Get up! Get up!" he shouted. "You cannot stay here!"

"But it is so nice," Ping said.

Tan Tan protested, "This is my tree! I own all of it: the trunk, the branches, the leaves, and the shade—everything!"

Ping thought, *I couldn't possibly buy all that, but maybe I could afford to buy the shade. And that might be even better.*

"Will you sell me the shade of the tree?" Ping asked Tan Tan.

Greedy Tan Tan loved money, and so he quickly answered,
"Why not?" thinking Ping was a silly goose.

Ping gave Tan Tan the two coins he had in his pocket, and the shade was sold.

Every day after that, Ping came to sit in the shade of the tree.

Wherever it happened to be, Ping sat in it.

When the shade moved into Tan Tan's big house,

so did Ping, with his chickens and his water buffalo.

When the shade moved into Tan Tan's bedroom,

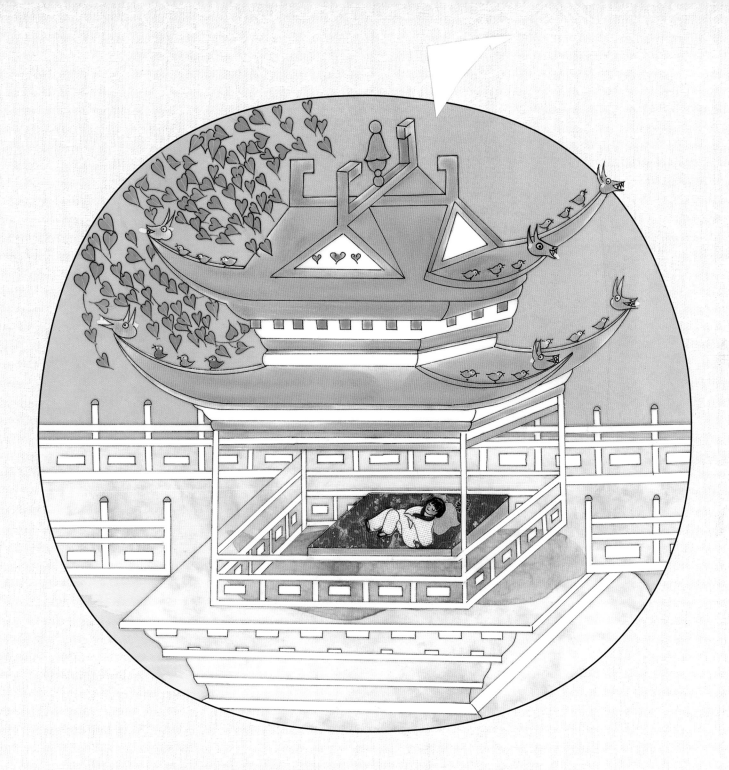

so did Ping, who took a nap right on Tan Tan's bed.

Often, Ping invited his many friends and their animals

to sit in the shade, too, wherever it happened to be.

A day came when Tan Tan could stand this no longer.

"How dare you come into my big house—and even into my
bedroom—with your animals and friends? Get out! Get out! Get
out!" he screamed.

But Ping continued as before, for he had bought the shade of the tree.

One day, Tan Tan was celebrating his birthday with his very rich friends. They were all seated around a big, shaded table when Ping suddenly entered riding his water buffalo and then sat down at the table, too.

When the friends learned that Tan Tan had sold the shade to Ping, they all laughed and said, "Tan Tan is a silly goose!"

This was too much for Tan Tan to bear.

He moved away to another house, where there was no shade and there were no trees . . .

and there were no friends.

Meanwhile, Ping noticed that the tree shaded some parts of the house all day and all night, too. And so he moved into the empty house, bringing his many friends and animals with him.

Ping never turned away anyone who wanted to rest or to sing
and dance in the beautiful shade of the shady tree.

Not even Tan Tan.